I Can Read!

BEGINNING
1
READING

Amelia Bedelia

·Makes a Friend·

D0317593

by **Herman Parish** ✽ pictures by **Lynne Avril**

Greenwillow Books, *An Imprint of* HarperCollins*Publishers*

Amelia Bedelia was lucky.

Her best friend lived next door.

"Hello, Jen!" said Amelia Bedelia.

"Hi, Amelia Bedelia!" said Jen.

Amelia Bedelia and Jen

had been friends

since they were babies.

They baked together.

They dressed up together.

They played music together.

Amelia Bedelia even showed Jen
how to bowl.

"They play so well together,"
said Amelia Bedelia's mother.
"They sure do," said Jen's mother.
"Even though they are
as different as night and day."

Then one day,

Jen and her parents

moved away.

Amelia Bedelia and her parents

were very sad.

Amelia Bedelia missed Jen.

She missed Jen every day.

She wished Jen would come back.

One morning, a moving van pulled up.

"Did Jen come back?"

asked Amelia Bedelia.

"I don't think so,"

said Amelia Bedelia's mother.

"We must have new neighbors."

Amelia Bedelia's mother
watched the movers.
"Oh, look," she said.
"I see a fancy footstool."

Amelia Bedelia did not look.
She wanted Jen back.

14

"Look!" said Amelia Bedelia's mother.

"I see a coffee table."

Amelia Bedelia still did not look.

She just kept drawing.

15

Amelia Bedelia's
mother said,
"I see some
big armchairs."

"I see a loveseat."

"I see a twin bed."

Finally, Amelia Bedelia looked
at Jen's old house.

Then she looked at her drawings.

"Our new neighbors sound strange,"
she said.

That night, Amelia Bedelia
told her dad
about the new neighbors.

18

He loved her pictures.

"Amazing!" her dad said.

"I hope they have a pool table."

The next morning,
Amelia Bedelia and her mother
baked blueberry muffins.

They took the muffins
next door.

A lady opened the door.

"Hello there," she said.

"My name is Mrs. Adams.

You must be my new neighbors."

"No," said Amelia Bedelia.

"We already live here.

You are my new neighbor."

"You know," said Mrs. Adams,

"I think both of us are right.

Do come in."

"Mmmm," Mrs. Adams said.

"What smells so good?"

"My mom does," said Amelia Bedelia.

"I don't wear perfume yet."

Jen's house looked different.

Every room was full of boxes.

"Welcome to my mess,"

said Mrs. Adams.

"I will live out of boxes for a while."

That sounded fun to Amelia Bedelia.

"Are the twins in their bed?"

asked Amelia Bedelia.

"My goodness," said Mrs. Adams.

"You have sharp eyes."

Amelia Bedelia hoped that was good.

"My twin grandchildren

will visit today," said Mrs. Adams.

"Their names are Mary and Marty."

The twins visited that afternoon.

"Our grandma is a lot of fun,"

they told Amelia Bedelia.

They were right!

It was great to have a friend

right next door again.

Amelia Bedelia and Mrs. Adams
baked together.

They dressed up together.

They played music together.

"They have so much fun together,"
said Amelia Bedelia's father.
"They sure do,"
said Amelia Bedelia's mother.
"Even though they are
as different as night and day."

One day Jen came back to visit.

Mrs. Adams took both girls

to a real bowling alley.

"This is the best day ever,"

said Amelia Bedelia.

"I have a best old friend

and a best new friend.

We are three best friends together!"